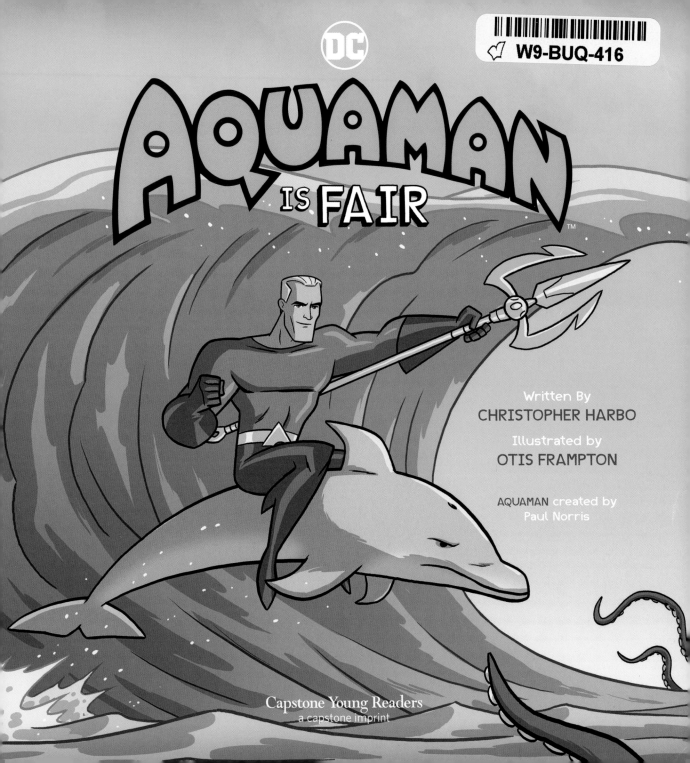

Aquaman is fair. He plays by the rules and shares with others. Everyone can trust him to treat people right.

When Aquaman plays a game, he always follows the rules.

The King of the Seven Seas is fair because he never cheats.

When Aquaman serves on a team, he uses all his skills to help.

Aquaman is fair because he does his share of the work.

When Aquaman shares a snack with his friends, he divides it evenly.

Aquaman is fair because he makes sure everyone gets an equal amount.

When Aquaman tackles a tough problem, he asks for advice.

Aquaman is fair because he listens to other people's ideas.

When Aquaman solves an argument, he listens to both sides.

The King of the Seven Seas is fair because he knows everyone's opinion is important.

When Aquaman battles evildoers, he makes sure they get what they deserve.

Aquaman is fair because his punishments fit the crimes.

When Aquaman causes an accident, he admits
that it was his fault.

Aquaman is fair because he doesn't blame others for his mistakes.

When Aquaman calls for backup, he includes everyone who wants to help.

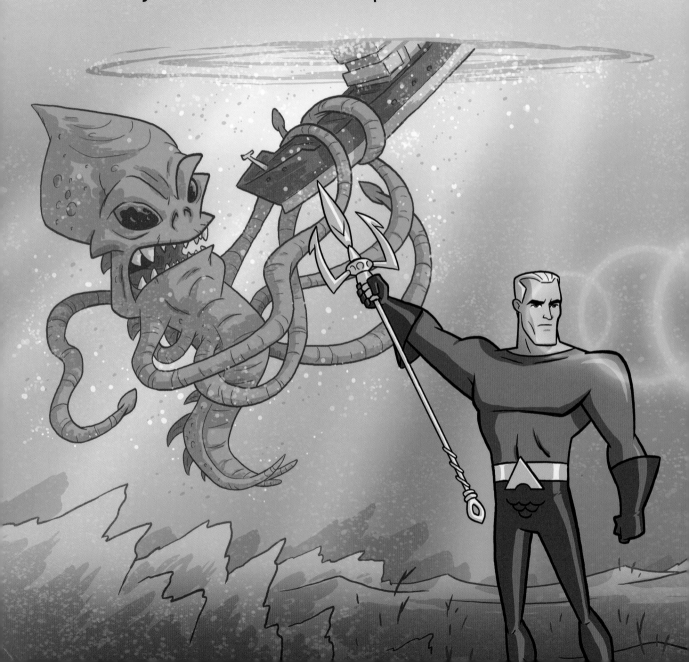

The King of the Seven Seas is fair because he doesn't leave anyone out.

Whenever super-villains attack, Aquaman rushes into battle like the rising tide.

And he always defeats them, fair and square!

AQUAMAN SAYS...

- Being fair means following the rules, like when I play games with my friends in Atlantis.

- Being fair means sharing things equally, like when I divide seaweed evenly between the sea turtles.

- Being fair means not blaming others for your mistakes, like when I admit that my whale accidentally crunched Batman's boat.

- Being fair means including everyone, like when I welcome sea life, large and small, to help me battle the Kraken.

- Being fair means being the best you that you can be!

BE YOUR BEST
with the World's Greatest Super Heroes!

ONLY FROM CAPSTONE!

DC Super Heroes Character Education
is published by Capstone Young Readers
A Capstone Imprint
1710 Roe Crest Drive
North Mankato, Minnesota 56003
www.mycapstone.com

Copyright © 2018 DC Comics.
AQUAMAN and all related characters and elements
are © & ™ DC Comics. WB SHIELD: ™ & © Warner Bros.
Entertainment Inc. (s18)

STAR40361

All rights reserved. No part of this publication may be
reproduced in whole or in part, or stored in a retrieval
system, or transmitted in any form or by any means,
electronic, mechanical, photocopying, recording, or
otherwise, without written permission of the publisher.

Editor: Julie Gassman
Designer: Hilary Wacholz
Art Director: Bob Lentz

Cataloging-in-Publication Data is available
at the Library of Congress website.

ISBN: 978-1-62370-954-9

Printed and bound in the USA.
010848S18